The Magic Door to Everywhere

Words by MAURITA COLEY FLIPPIN

Pictures by LINAY ASHLEIGH LITTLE

The story herein represents fictional characters drawn upon the experiences of the author, Maurita Coley Flippin, and original pictures drawn by artist Linay Ashleigh Little.

Discounts are available for books ordered in bulk, and when ordering for a speaking engagement with the author.

For permission or discounts, contact:
info@mauritacoley.com
Twitter: @MauritaColey.com
https://www.linkedin.com/in/mauritacoley/
https://www.facebook.com/maurita.coley

Printed in the United States of America.

DEDICATION

This book is dedicated to our family's matriarch Essie L. Harris, aka "Bigma" for her 101-plus years of love, life, grace, and fantastic stories.

This book is based on a true story; it was originally published as a short story on the website of the Gabriel Richard Branch Library in Detroit, Michigan under the title *"Gabriel Richard's Secrets of Survival."*

It is inspired by and dedicated to the author's fond memories of the Gabriel Richard Branch Library, Detroit, Michigan, and the McGregor Public Library, Highland Park, Michigan, both of which are closed and boarded up as of this writing. May their magic doors of opportunity soon open to inspire generations today and to come.

ACKNOWLEDGMENTS

The writer would like to acknowledge all of the people who inspired this book along the many years of its journey from the author's experience as a young girl to sharing it with a digital generation. Many thanks to my writing coach Clyde "Baba Kojo" McElvene, co-founder and former executive director of the Hurston-Wright Foundation, for helping me to feel as if this is a story still worth telling after so many years, and who inspired me to allow my niece, Linay Ashleigh Little, to use her artistic gifts to illustrate the story; and to Linda Gill Anderson, former colleague at BET Books who used her valuable time and talents to help me get it to the finish line. To my parents, Mattie Coley and Sandy Coley, Sr., who endured, and actually grew to love, their daughter's obsession with libraries; and to my four brothers Sandy Jr., Mark, Derick, and Troy, who allowed themselves to be dragged along. To my dear friends Maureen Lewis, Angela Brown, Donna Daley, Yvonne Bennett, Terry Johnson, Irene Albritton, Eloise Foster, Rachelle Viki Brown, Loretta Polk, Ulysses Little, Celeste Garcia, Dr. Yvonne Bolling, my sisters-in-law Merle Flippin Cumberbatch and Christine Gaydu Coley, and to numerous other friends who encouraged me, and who assured me that my "library story" is still relevant today. And last, but far from least, to my husband and fellow writer, Paul Flippin who met me long after this story was conceived but who fans the fires of my obsessions and tolerates the daily frustrations of living with a writer who does everything...but writ

"…More than a building that houses books and data, the library represents a window to a larger world…"
--Barack Obama, Democratic U.S. senator from Illinois, excerpt from keynote address of the Opening General Session at the ALA Annual Conference, Chicago, IL, June 25-29, 2005
https://americanlibrariesmagazine.org/bound-to-the-word/#interview

CONTENTS

1 - THE PROMISE

Ms. Lake tried to comfort screaming Markie as Mr. Lake stormed into the living room in rumpled pajamas, and a rumpled voice to match.

"Mommie, somebody broke my truck!" wailed four-year old Benny, his huge eyes dropping tears on his pajamas in big splats; his heaving sobs a clear indicator that it was naptime. Markie's wails intensified, and Benny wailed right along in harmony and sympathy; they make a pitiful duet, waking their two older two brothers Jemar and Jordan who yelled in protest from their rooms.

"Louise!" Sandy Lake sounded weary as he appeared at the threshold to the living room. "Honey, can you get the kids to stop all the noise! I need to get some sleep - you know I'm working the night shift this week." Frustrated and sleepy, Daddy Lake sounded as if he felt like crying himself.

"Clarke, can you come and help me with the kids," asked Mom Lake as she cradled crying Markie in her arms.

Clarke looked up from her book, oblivious to all the chaos.

"But Mom –," she whined. "I've been *waiting all morning*. It's Saturday—we're supposed to go to the library, *remember?*"

"Okay, Honey, I know it's your turn," Louise said in a tired, weary voice. "I know what I promised, and I don't want to disappoint you. But I can't take you to the library right now—I've got my hands full with the boys."

Clarke's eyes welled up with tears. Boys were such trouble! Jemar and Jordan could have helped with the little kids, but they stayed in bed with the covers over their heads. Just because she was the oldest it seemed expected that she had these responsibilities. She was just a kid herself!

The promise was being broken, Clarke pouted, and it just wasn't fair. Clarke's father was supposed to watch Clarke's four brothers while her mother drove her to the library on Saturday mornings. But after Daddy Lake lost his job as a brick mason, he had to work several jobs just to make ends meet. Sometimes, Clarke could hear her parents discussing the bills late at night as she read her library books under the covers with a flashlight.

Daddy Lake's night job ended her parents' late night discussions over money, but it meant everyone had to be quiet during the day while Daddy slept. This didn't bother Clarke one bit because, whether chaos or calm reigned in the Lake household, she always had a book in her hand taking her anywhere and everywhere she wanted – taking her far away from it all.

"I don't need this," muttered Clarke angrily. Disgusted, she stormed out of the living room, grabbing an armful of library books as she headed out of the house. She flung open the front screened door of her family's neat yellow brick home and slammed it shut with a splat.

Dodging toys that were strewn all over the yard, she ran across the lawn, grabbed her old yellow bike, dumped the books into the basket on the bike's handlebars and pedaled off.

"I don't need anyone; I can take care of myself," she muttered as she took off down the street.

Clarke pedaled furiously down Hillsboro Street, rolling past her friendly neighbors without her usual greeting. Some waved, some look at her quizzically and continued their yard work before the heat from the unseasonably hot Detroit summer sun overcame them.

"Hi Clarke," waved Miss Ayo as she watered her beautiful lawn. "You off to the library again? Good for *you!*"

"Morning Clarke, where's the fire!" joked Mr. McDermott as she approached him, working in his garden.

Clarke waved but pedaled on faster.

"Whoa, slow down, Baby Girl"— teased Mr. McDermott as she flew past him—"those books ain't goin' no where!"

She pedaled on, through several blocks of the modest but tidy homes and well-manicured patches of lawn as she approached the main intersection, Grand River Avenue.

2 - UNFAMILIAR TERRITORY

On Grand River Avenue, the friendly neighbors and their Hillsboro Street homes faded into the distance, replaced by store fronts and office buildings. Clarke saw customers chatting and drinking coffee outside as she pedaled past a neighborhood laundromat. A man swept the sidewalk in front of a beauty salon as ladies waited inside to get their hair done; he stepped aside quickly to let Clarke pass.

In the next block, Clarke rode past a stretch of buildings that were dilapidated and boarded up. Exercising care to avoid broken glass and litter strewn on her path, she realized she had only been on this street in the comfort and safety of the family car and had never seen it close-up.

For the first time, she noticed how run down and empty some of the buildings on this block looked. She rode by a gas station with broken signs and peeling paint that looked abandoned. What had been a bakery and a flower shop, looked deserted and downright scary.

A man sat on the ground leaning against a building that used to be the neighborhood dry cleaner; the windows were boarded up. His tousled blanket, a backpack, and some leftover food wrappers were strewn in the doorway. He tipped his cap as Clarke approached him; smiled a friendly, toothless grin, and reached out to offer her a sip of whatever was inside a brown paper bag. Clarke cycled along, picking up speed.

The ride seemed to take forever; when Mom drove her, it didn't seem to be far at all, and definitely not scary like it felt today. She sped up.

The books almost fell out of the basket as her bike hit bump after bump. The sidewalk was an obstacle course of potholes, so she looked downward to carefully avoid riding right into one of them!

Suddenly, she looked up and saw a group of boys in her path just ahead. She squinted through her glasses to see if there was a familiar face in the bunch. She hated boys; they were nothing but trouble, always playing tricks. She should never have run off like that, she thought, making the trip to the library all alone. She was a long way from Hillsboro Street now, with the library nowhere in sight and a group of unknown boys on her path. For a moment, she considered turning back, or crossing the street to evade the group that showed no sign of parting to let her through.

Instead, she barreled ahead, secretly hoping for an escape route.

3 - FALLING DOWN

As she got closer, the boys finally gave way to let her through. But just then, a hand reached out and grabbed her handlebars, and she felt a hard shove from behind her seat. Clarke, the bicycle and the books sailed off in different directions.

Clarke landed on the sidewalk with a thud before sliding off the curb, into the street where she came to a stop, sandwiched between two parked cars. Her eyeglasses had flown off and now perched dangerously near the gutter; her bike was wedged under a car bumper . Her right hand and knee stung with pain after cutting her knee on a piece of broken glass.

The boys laughed hysterically, bouncing a basketball between them as they continued on their way.

"Ooops! You better watch where you're going four eyes. Whatcha doing with all those books anyway? Why don't you get a iPad or somethin'—nobody be readin' no *books*!"

"And tell your daddy to get you a new bike—that one is embarrassing!!"

Clarke could not see their faces without her glasses, but she noticed one of th boys had on a Detroit Pistons jersey and matching "Bad Boys" cap. She could hear them in the distance now, still laughing and bouncing their ball.

"Come on Anu, let's go play some ball," said one of the boys.

Clarke scrambled to get back up, retrieving her books and glasses before they slid out of reach into the gutter. She could hear the boys' laughter taunting her from afar. Angry and humiliated, she fought back tears realizing she had to go back home, her bold journey now a failed attempt at independence.

But as she got up, she saw her destination – the Gabriel Richard Branch Library: it was right across the street, on the other side of the busy Grand River intersection. It had seemed so far away, but there it was, right in front of her, as if welcoming her to come in. Tears stung her eyes as she dusted herself off and collected her books. A small trickle of blood ran down her right knee and stained her sock. She grabbed her bike, straightened the handlebars defiantly, and continued her journey, with determination.

4 - GETTING BACK UP

As she waited for the cross-light to change, Clarke's spirits soared; this was her very first visit to Gabriel Richard Library all alone! Mom would be so proud! Suddenly, she felt ashamed at her disrespectful outburst towards her mother – she should not have run off like that, Mom would be worried. But she cherished her Saturday morning visits to the library, and Mom had broken her promise to take her.

The good thing was that now she knew she could take *herself* to the library and make things easier on Mom. And as much as her little brothers got on her nerves, she could be more patient with them and help around the house more. Dad would get a better job soon, and they would all be happy again.

And it really wasn't a long way to the library after all. She had her bicycle, and in the winter, she could take the bus.

Clarke had not seen him, but the boy in the Detroit Pistons jersey and cap had lingered behind the others, watching her as she gathered her belongings while the other boys continued on to their destination. He seemed uncertain, as if he were not sure whether he should help Clarke, or follow his friends.

After Clarke rode off on her bike, he noticed what looked like a book underneath a car near where she had fallen. He walked over and scooped up the book; the cover featured a boy about his age, who even looked like him. *Bud, Not Buddy*, was the title. What a surprise, he thought, as he flipped through the pages. He would not have expected a girl to read a book like this.

Fascinated, he read as he walked.

10

5 - CROSSING THE GRAND RIVER

Clarke walked her bike across Grand River Avenue; she was very proud of herself. And Mom would be proud of her too, after scolding her determined daughter for leaving without a word.

Arriving at the library, she locked her bike in the bike rack, collected the books from the basket, and confidently climbed the steps to Gabriel Richard Library's welcoming double doors.

Ms. Phillips, her favorite librarian, greeted her at the door. Noticing her disheveled appearance, Ms. Phillips frowned with concern.

"Hi Clarke," Ms. Phillips asked kindly. "Are you alright…".

"Yes!" Clarke assured her. "I just fell off my bike and twisted my glasses. Guess I'll have to ask my dad to get me some new glasses now!" she teased. "Maybe a new bike too!"

"Well, as long as you're okay…." said Ms. Phillips, still a bit concerned. "By the way, Atlantis Browder has a new book! It's called *Africa on My Mind*. Remember you read her first book, *My First Trip to Africa*, a few years ago? This new book is all about her second trip to Egypt in Africa. It's in the World History and Culture section when you are ready to check out."

"Thanks Ms. Phillips!" Clarke beamed at the thought of a new book. At the front desk, Clarke waited patiently as Ms. Phillips scanned the books she had returned. *Mufaro's Beautiful Daughters*, by John Steptoe, *Island of the Blue Dolphins*, by Scott O'Dell; *The Alchemist*, by Paolo Coelho; *Sasha Savvy Loves to Code*, by Sasha Ariel Alston. Thanks to Ms. Phillips' suggestions, Clarke's hunger for knowledge had introduced her to stories about people from all over the world.

As sad as Clarke was to return these books whose characters had been her friends for the past week, Clarke was excited about the new friends that awaited her in the stacks. As she waited for Ms. Phillips to scan her books, she stood in the archway in anticipation as the stacks loomed all around her.

"Clarke, did you forget one of your books?" asked Ms. Phillips. "*Bud, Not Buddy*, by Christopher Paul Curtis is missing. Do you think you left it at home?"

Puzzled, Clarke returned to the desk. "I thought it was there; I had it with me…".

Outside, the boy with the Detroit Pistons jersey and cap stopped at the front steps of the Library, a book gripped tightly in his hand. He hesitated momentarily, looking around as if he were worried that his friends might see him going into a library. Then he proceeded up the steps, opened the wide door, and stepped into to a new world.

Mesmerized, as he entered, he looked up at the soaring ceilings as the sun beamed through an atrium and through floor to ceiling windows, casting beams of light and illuminating shelves and shelves of – *books*. He closed his eyes as the brightness and energy of this place stimulated every one of his senses. He felt as if he could even taste something magical in this place.

"There it is!" yelled Clarke, pointing accusingly at the book in the boy's hand. Startled, the boy stood frozen in his tracks.

6 IN THE STACKS

"Come on in young man – welcome to Gabriel Richard Library. I haven't seen you here before—what's your name?" probed Ms. Phillips.

The boy and Clarke glared at each other. Finally, he looked down, as if contemplating his next move, and he slowly stepped forward.

"Anu," said the boy shyly, in response to Ms. Phillips. "She dropped this book when she fell off her bike, so I followed her here." He watched Clarke warily, as if he assumed she would tell about the incident with the bike.

"Hmmph!" snarled Clarke. "It's not as if I fell off my bike all by myself. I had *help*! That's why I hate *boys*."

Ms. Phillips saw an opportunity to do her favorite thing in the world: to invite another child through the magic door to everywhere.

"Well Anu," Ms. Phillips said with a smile. "Thank you so

much for finding the book and bringing it to us. You just walked through what we call 'the magic door to everywhere.' Once you come through that magic door, you can travel anywhere you want to go, meet anyone you want to meet, or learn anything you want to know. The only price is your agreement to return the books when they are due."

"I didn't know libraries had computers!" said Anu in awe of the line of new computers and printers he saw.

"Yes we do! You are welcome to use any of our 25 computers to locate anything you don't find here in the library. We have 40,000 books here. Are you interested in the book Clarke is returning? The author, Christopher Paul Curtis, was born right over in Flint, Michigan! He has written some great books and comes here on occasion to read to the children. –Do you have a library card?

"Well," said Clarke sarcastically, unable to believe that this awful boy is invading her special space and shifting her favorite librarian's attention to him, "he doesn't need a library card; he probably can't even *read.*"

Ms. Phillips frowned, not sure how to take Clarke's apparent anger. Sensing an opportunity to smooth things over, he had an idea.

"Clarke comes here every Saturday morning; she knows the stacks like the back of her hand," Ms. Phillips continued with her sales pitch.

"And if you're 12, we can get you your own library card and you can check out that book right now," continued Ms. Phillips. "Or if you're not 12 yet, you can have your parents sign for you to have a card. You can even check out books electronically, through an app on your smartphone. And we also have tutors that can help you with homework if you need help."

"Clarke, how about showing Anu around the stacks?" urged Ms. Phillips.

Grudgingly, Clarke glared at Anu, then shrugged and beckoned for him to follow her.

Anu followed Clarke into a wide-open room where books lined the shelves from floor to ceiling. I wondered why they called it "the stacks," he thought to himself, reluctant to ask Clarke to explain it to him in her current state of – rude. In an open area near the stacks, lots of sparkling new computers and printers lined the room in individual cubbies.

"What kind of stupid name is that – A-noo?" sneered Clarke as he complied with Ms. Phillips' request to show Anu around. "A new what? I never heard of a name like that." She wasn't done with this guy yet, he would pay for what he and his friends had done to her.

"It's *Anu,*" corrected the boy. "And it's not a stupid name, or 'a new' name. I was named after the African god also known as Anubis. When a person in ancient Egypt died, Anubis measured the kindness of a person's heart to determine whether they would go to heaven. My uncle showed me the whole story in a book called *Nile Valley Contributions to Civilization*; I bet you never even heard of it."

Slightly impressed, Clarke continued to act aloof.

"And anyway, what kind of name is Clarke, especially for a girl," Anu jeered; he was not going to be intimidated by a girl.

"*I'm* named after Dr. John Henrik *Clarke*, a great Black

thinker, educator, author and historian," boasted Clarke. "And I'll bet you've never even heard of *him* either. In fact, have you ever even read a book, by anybody?"

"I have read plenty of books," countered Anu; "I've just never been inside a *library*."

7 THE MAGIC DOOR TO EVERYWHERE

"You've never been inside a *library*?" asked Clarke, incredulously. She raised one eyebrow at this boy, instantly judging him. "Well," she bragged, "I come to the library every Saturday and I'm going to read *all* of the books here. I'm only in the 6th grade, and my teacher says I'm reading on the 11th grade reading level!"

"I'm in the 6th grade too, and *my* teacher said I'm reading on the *12th* grade reading level," said Anu, triumphantly. "And I've never been to a library, but I read all the time."

Clarke's eyes widened in amazement at this news. She had really misjudged this boy, because of the other boys he was hanging out with, and because of what they did to her. And maybe even because of what he was wearing, and how he wore his cap, she just assumed he wasn't a reader.

Detecting her change in attitude about him, Anu added, "I read a lot, just on the internet."

The two children looked at one another, then finally laughed. Despite their different backgrounds, and the unfortunate circumstances of their meeting, they obviously had one big thing in common – they shared a love for reading.

"Why were you hanging out with those boys?" asked Clarke, more politely this time. "They don't look like they've ever seen a book, let alone read one."

"Well, I didn't want to say anything in front of that lady, but I'm really sorry about the bike," said Anu, apologetically. "We only talked about blocking your way, for fun, I didn't know we would make you fall. Plus, I don't really like hanging out with Troy and Ryan anymore. I always seem to get in trouble when I'm with them. They're not bad boys, really. We used to be the math games champions at Pattengill Elementary School. Then when we got to sixth grade, they thought it was boring and they just wanted to start doing silly stuff. I guess I just followed along."

Clarke, stunned by Anu's apology, was really impressed now. Her younger brother Jemar only apologized to her when forced by their parents. Maybe all boys weren't so bad after all.

"Well, this is a great place to bring them to hang out," advised Clarke. "And reading on the computer is fine; but being in the library, and reading a real book with real pages, to me is like – magic. And being with other people who love reading is a great way to spend the day!"

Anu nodded in agreement, looking around, he saw adults and children reading quietly around shared tables. In a corner of the library, preschoolers huddled around a teacher as she read out loud to them. To his surprise, he realized that he felt very comfortable here.

Ms. Phillips smiled at the children from the front desk.

"Come on, Anu," Clarke motioned. "Welcome to the magic door to everywhere; let's go find you a great book!

Clarke's Questions for Reading Circles

1. What are some key examples of symbolism in this book?
2. What character traits contrast/separate Clarke from her antagonist? What traits do they have in common?
3. How does Clarke's family life shape her independence and her fears?
4. Describe your first trip to a library. Did you check out a book?
5. What did you learn from Clarke's character?
6. What did you learn from Anu's character?
7. How do Anu's life experiences shape his opinions about reading, and about books?
8. Who is your favorite character in this book, and why?
9. Have you read any of the books on Clarke's reading list?
10. What is your favorite book?

Recommended Reading

Below is a list of some of Clarke's favorite books for middle grade readers, and above.

1. Slam Dunk! By Sharon Robinson
2. Sasha Savvy Loves to Code, by Sasha Ariel Alston
3. The Alchemist, by Paolo Coelho
4. Mufaro's Beautiful Daughters, by John Steptoe
5. The Watsons Go to Birmingham, by Christopher Paul Curtis
6. Bud, Not Buddy, by Christopher Paul Curtis
7. Nile Valley Contributions to Civilization, by Anthony T. Browder
8. Bookspeak by Laura Purdie Salas
9. The Life of Paul Robeson, by Eloise Greenfield
10. Brown Girl Dreaming, by Jacqueline Woodson
11. The Little Prince, by Antoine de Saint Exupery
12. Africa on My Mind, by Alexis Browder

ABOUT THE AUTHOR

MAURITA COLEY FLIPPIN is a lawyer, nonprofit executive, and former media executive for the Black Entertainment Television Networks. She is passionate about writing and amplifying stories that empower people to achieve their dreams. She earned a Bachelor of Arts in Communications from Michigan State University, and a Juris Doctor from the Georgetown University Law Center where she has received the top alumni awards. She was acknowledged by BlackWomenTech.com as one of 200 Black Women in Tech to Follow on Twitter. She is a dedicated member of the Metropolitan African Methodist Episcopal Church in Washington, DC, and of the Daniel Alexander Payne Community Development Corporation where she helps to produce events that empower the community.

Maurita is a native of Detroit, Michigan and the oldest of five children and the only daughter. This book was inspired by and based on a true story of the numerous hours she spent at the Gabriel Richard Public Library in Detroit and the McGregor Memorial Public Library in Highland Park, Michigan, often dragging her little brothers along with her. Maurita lives in Washington D.C. with her husband, Paul Flippin, a retired firefighter and emergency management leader at the University of Maryland, who is also a writer.

This is Maurita's first published children's book. She is a co-author of *How to Start an Investment Club* with Irene Albritton and T. Eloise Foster.

You can follow Maurita Coley Flippin on Twitter @MauritaColey

ABOUT THE ILLUSTRATOR

LINAY ASHLEIGH LITTLE was, at the time of these illustrations, a rising sixth grader and consistent Honor Roll student at Scripps Middle School in Lake Orion, Michigan. Linay loves to write, read, and draw, and she has a passion for reading, especially literary classics. As of 2019, Linay is a Junior at Lake Orion High School, and enjoys reading, art, and editing her own future novels.

Quotes about Libraries

Link to a podcast about a true story of a man who "stole" library books as a child, and who grows up to become an attorney. He learns many years later at a class reunion that the librarians planted the books he had stolen when they realized he was interested in reading.
https://www.npr.org/templates/story/story.php?storyId=113357239?storyId=113357239

"My alma mater was books, a good library... I could spend the rest of my life reading, just satisfying my curiosity."
—Malcolm X

"For a person who grew up in the '30's and the '40's in the segregated South, with so many doors closed without explanation to me, libraries and books said, 'Here I am, read me.'"
—Maya Angelou

"Reading is important. Books are important. Librarians are important. Also, libraries are not child-care facilities, but sometimes feral children raise themselves among the stacks."
—Neil Gaiman

"She tried to act as though it were nothing to go to the library alone. But her happiness betrayed her."
—Maud Hart Lovelace, *Betsy and Tacy Go Downtown*

"When I graduated from high school, it was during the Depression and we had no money. I couldn't go to college, so I went to the library three days a week for 10 years."
—Ray Bradbury

Made in the USA
Monee, IL
09 September 2019